Dexter Carleton Washburn

Songs from the Seasons, and Other Verses

Dexter Carleton Washburn

Songs from the Seasons, and Other Verses

ISBN/EAN: 9783337181956

Printed in Europe, USA, Canada, Australia, Japan

Cover: Foto ©Andreas Hilbeck / pixelio.de

More available books at **www.hansebooks.com**

SONGS

FROM THE SEASONS

And Other Verses

BY

DEXTER CARLETON WASHBURN

𝔖econd 𝔈dition

ST. JOHNSBURY
CHARLES T. WALTER
1888

PREFACE.

THE enjoyment the author has taken in composing these Songs, and the pleasure they might give his friends, have been his only reasons for writing them; the hope that they may give to their readers, in some degree, a similar pleasure, is his only excuse for publishing them.

Some of these verses have never appeared in type before; several of them have been published in St. Nicholas, Outing, The Cottage Hearth, Literary Life, and other magazines and periodicals.

D. C. W.

CHRISTMAS, 1886.

2

NOTE.

SOME slight changes have been made in the present edition, and a few verses added.

D. C. W.

CHRISTMAS, 1887.

CONTENTS.

I

SONGS FROM THE SEASONS.

WINTER:

PAGE

A Christmas Carol . . . 15
A Christmas Wish 16
A Valentine 17
My Little Saint 18
Horace, Book I. Ode IX . . 21
Sweeping out the School-House Floor 23
Last Night 25
The Lamplighter 27
Tableaux 29

SPRING:

Easter Morning 33
Sunday Morning 34
Elizabeth 36
My Blotter 37
Jen 40
The Songs I do not Sing . . 41

SUMMER:

Down by the Brook 44

Daisies 46

Lines, Written on a Birch-Bark Cup 47

A Letter 48

My Tennis Hat 50

My Polo Cap 51

AUTUMN:

An Autumn Hymn 55

Flowers 56

Inspiration 58

A Cloudy Morning in the Country . 60

The Angelus Bell 62

A Birthday Wish 64

Ode for the night before a birthday . 65

II

OTHER VERSES.

Just a Society Girl 73

Saint Valentine's Day . . . 77

With a MS. Book 79

Lost Youth 81

Evening on the Harbor . . . 83

Baby's Socks 85

Easter Day 87
Cards 89
Echo 91
No Go 92
A Remembrance 93
Remembrances 95
Why 97
Ivy Ode 98
Fetters 100
"Sweet Caporal" 103
A Puff of Smoke 105
The Seasons 107
The Poet and the Singer . . 109
Life's Day 114
Colors 115
Chivalry 116
I Wonder 117

1

SONGS FROM THE SEASONS

A CHRISTMAS CAROL.

MERRILY ring the Christmas chimes,
As they merrily rang in the olden times ;
For hearts grown sad and heads grown gray
Are young once more on Christmas-day.

Cheerily blazes the Christmas fire
On the old stone hearth, as the flames mount
higher ;
For children that long have learned to stray
Come home again on Christmas-day.

Joyously echoes the Christmas song
Of youthful voices, clear and strong ;
For "Peace on Earth, good-will" was given
To the sons of men from the Son of Heaven.

A CHRISTMAS WISH.

MAY the Christmas chime
   Bring a thought of the time
When the heavens rang with a song sublime.

Though the closing year
Be dark and drear,
May the new one dawn on you bright and clear.

A VALENTINE.

"WHO is your Valentine?" asked she :
"A dainty maiden," answered he.

"Of course ; but is she fair?" said she :
"As fair as your own self," quoth he.

"And are her eyes bright?" still asked she :
"I' faith, they are my stars," said he.

"What may I tell her by?" said she :
"The dimple in her cheek," spoke he.

"I have one, too ; what else?" laughed she :
"Her maiden's heart, so true," quoth he.

"Oh, pshaw ! who is this maid?" cried she :
"You are my Valentine," said he.

MY LITTLE SAINT.

HER picture stands here in my study,
   On a shelf, by an overgrown book,
Where the curtain, drawn back from the window,
   Makes just the right kind of a nook—

For a Saint who appears somewhat worldly,
   With her kids, and her velvet, and furs,
And a Gainsborough hat, and whose tresses
   Are as stylishly "frizzled" as hers.

Of course it is only a picture,—
   And fancy at that: but who cares!
And the legend below, "Come and kiss me,"
   Isn't what a Saint usually bears:

But still I have made her the patron
   Of all that I write, say, or do :—
I call her "Saint Dimple Cheek,"—really
   I think that sounds classic, don't you?

And here, through the long winter evenings,
  As I sit with my papers and books,
Leaning back in my low wooden rocker,
  My little saint smilingly looks.

And here, every evening, my candle,
  (And the paper shade, too, sometimes,) burns,
On my little saint's dim, curtained altar,
  Till her hair to a bright halo turns.

But still I'll confess that the worship
  I pay, is not wholly unmixed ;
In fact, that quite often upon her
  'Tis my eyes, not my thoughts, that are fixed.

And, that, as the faithful believer
  Who kneels by an image to pray,
Prays not to the image, but worships
  The spirit it figures, alway :—

So I, at my little saint's altar,
  See not there the face in her niche,
But smilingly think of another
  Just such a demure little witch,—

Who once said the picture was "pretty,"
    And then, of course, had to demur,
When I acquiesced promptly, and hinted
    I thought it was very like her.

Well, well, I must be at my reading,
    Not sitting here wasting my time :
She would laugh,—and—well, just to amuse her,
    I think I must send her my rhyme !

HORACE—BOOK I. ODE IX.

SEE Soracte's dazzling glow,
Covered deep in virgin snow!
While the laboring forests stand
Bowing to the grateful land;
And the river's glistening band
Is congealed.

Banish cold! and on the hearth
Pile the logs with social mirth:
Thaliarchus, draw the wine,
Mellowed on the Sabine vine;
And in ancient jar of thine
Long concealed.

Trust the gods with all thy cares:
They the storm-winds, waging wars
With the billows dark and cold,
Will control, and safe withhold,
Cypress tall nor ashes old
To disturb.

4

What to-morrow's grief shall be
Strive not ere the time to see :
If to Fortune thou should'st climb
Count it so much gained of Time ;
Neither Youth's romantic rhyme
    Try to curb.

Ere old age comes, all too soon,
Beat the dance to jovial tune :
Seek the green, and gayly rove
Midst soft murmurings of love,
While the twilight stars above
    Mark the hour.

Hear the maid's betraying laugh,
By the wall concealed but half !
Seize a love-pledge from her hand,
Or her white arm's golden band :
See her, laughing, coyly stand
    In your power !

SWEEPING OUT THE SCHOOL-HOUSE FLOOR.

I'D dismissed the "class in spelling"
    Quite a little while before,
And we'd just gone through our "parsing"
    As the short hand got to four.

Then the "big girls" started homeward,
    Chatting round the open door ;
But I stayed and helped Miss 'Villa
    While she swept the school-house floor.

Down the aisles our busy brooms went,
    And the dirt flew out before,
Till we made a mammoth dust-heap
    Just behind the entry door.

And I told her how we students
    Managed things at "Thirty-four,"—
Once a term we made the bed up,
    And the next term swept the floor !

While our hands and tongues were busy,
    As I glanced the benches o'er,
"What a pretty maiden," thought I,
    "Sweeping out the school-house floor ;"

"Such plump arms and graceful ankles,
    Faith, I never saw before ;
Bless me, isn't this romantic,
    Sweeping out the school-house floor !"

Then she bade me bring the dust-pan,
    Hanging up behind the door ;
And expertly swept the dirt in,
    While I held it on the floor.

Then she quickly tied her hood on,
    While I locked the school-house door,
And I left her at the corner,—
    Thus we swept the school-house floor !

LAST NIGHT.

I T was here that we were standing
In the party's whirl, last night;
Leaning on the polished newel,
As it shone beneath the light.

And I laughed, and called him "silly"
To be talking so, right here:
He could call on me some evening,
In,—perhaps,—well—say a year!

But I felt a twinge of conscience
As I left him standing there,
With his face so sad and weary,
And that earnest, thoughtful air.

Then, to-night, this train disaster!
All the evening paper's filled
With those cruel "press dispatches:"—
His name's in the list of "killed."

Oh, if I could but have known it   ·
    When he spoke to me last night,
I'd have answered him in earnest,
    Not in words so hard and light.

There! do hear it! it's a caller,—
    Oh, I *can't* see one to-night!
I have stood here thinking, dreaming
    Till my hair's a perfect fright.

Oh, I'm caught,—I hear them coming!—
    I'm not in, James,—see my head!
Mr. Who, James What? Tom Fielding?—
    Hush, man,—don't you know?—he's dead.

"Not quite dead yet?"—Oh, Tom Fielding,
    Is it really you,—alive?
"Just escaped?—with one arm broken?—
    You were one of only five?

May you make your call this evening?"
    It was here last night, at ten,
I said No: but,—don't you really
    Think its been a year since then?

THE LAMPLIGHTER.

U P here in my room
   Where the evening gloom
Is thickening the shadows fast,
   I sit by the side
   Of my window wide,
As the snow goes whirling past.

   Each shadowy fold
   That the curtains hold
Is lost in the deepening shades ;
   And familiar things
   Take fanciful wings
As the waning twilight fades.

   Outside, and below,
   The drifting snow
Goes whirling and eddying round ;
   And the wintry blast
   Is whistling past
With a weird and ghostly sound.

But up the street,
With shuffling feet,
Comes the lamplighter's muffled form ;
The ruddy light
Of his torch-lamp bright
Gleams red through the driving storm.

But a moment is lost
As he stops by the post,
Then he trudges along up the hill ;
But the flickering glare
That his torch left there
Through the storm is brightening still.

And well for me,
I think, would it be,
As I toil up life's stormy hill,
If I could but light
Some beacon bright
In the storm, that should brighten still.

TABLEAUX.

M^Y sweet little nun, with the soft, pretty face,
    Forgive me, I pray, but your black hood's
    white border
And your ribbons show there ;—may I put them
    in place,
Without breaking the rules of your sisterhood's
    order ?
There, that is just right,—so the kerchief will
    show
Inside of your nun's hood, or whatever this is ;
But, Santa Maria ! why, this never'll do,—
Don't you know, Sister Martha, black nuns don't
    wear frizzes?

I really am shocked at such folly and sin ;
Let me brush them back, so, from your fore-
    head and temples ;
O, dear, now you've pulled the hood off from
    your chin ;

Whoever did see a black nun with such dim-
     ples!
You really must let your hood cover them, so.
Look meek,—now look down,—there, that's
     perfect!—"you'll smother?"
But other black nuns have been roasted, you
     know;
'Tis but little to have a silk handkerchief bother.

Look as though you were thinking of all your
     bad deeds;
But here, what is this?—you must cover that
     locket,
And those rings on your hand.   "Must be tell-
     ing your beads?"
Well, then, off with them, quick; here they go,
     in my pocket.
And now let me see how you'll walk;—very
     slow;

Ah! that was well done; and—but here, stop
     that switching!
And if you *could* manage to be,—well, you
     know,
To be just a little less,—O, less bewitching,—

'Twould be better, I think. But what's this that
you say?—
"Don't believe you *can* learn? Let them go on
without you?"—
My dear Sister Martha, now don't pout that
way;
You know I don't mention the good things about
you.

.   .   .   .

She has gone through the archway,—the scene
has begun:
What a lucky chap he who may ever possess
her;
I' faith, if there was such a fair little nun
It would be a hard chance for her Father Con-
fessor.
I fear it would scatter his Latin and Greek
If he once caught a glimpse of the sweet little
sister.
What a rumpus she'd make! Ere she'd been
there a week,
I'd swear every monk in the convent had kissed
her!

L'ENVOY.

Well, that was last night, and the tableaux are
    done ;
But still, as I take down the stage and the awn-
    ing,
The thought of my sweet-faced, demure little
    nun
Brings a smile to my lips in the midst of my
    yawning.

EASTER MORNING.

DELICATE perfumes, faint and rare,
Floating like dreams in the soft spring air :

Radiant lilies, pure and white,
Opening their hearts in the morning light :

Glorious beams from the Easter sun :
Glorious news from the Risen One.

SUNDAY MORNING.

THROUGH the painted, pictured windows,
  Comes a flood of mellow light,
Warming up the shadowy transepts
  With its colors rich and bright.

And from out the distant chancel
  Comes the service floating down,
As the preacher slowly reads it
  In his rustling stole and gown.

But my thoughts are sadly wandering
  From the solemn and the grand ;
And I scarcely keep the places
  Through the prayer-book in my hand.

For there sits a dainty maiden
  Just across the long straight aisle,
With a pious little look on,
  And a most bewitching smile.

And she sings like Saint Cecilia,
   Till the roof the music feels,
And the sombre oaken rafters,
   As the chants the organ peals.

And, at last, the service ended
   With a burst of rapturous song,
From the pulpit comes a sermon,—
   Strange, I find it none too long!

Then the peaceful benediction,
   And the organ swells once more :
While without the porch I linger
   Till I meet her at the door.

ELIZABETH.

LASHES long, o'er laughing eyes
      Vainly trying to look wise ;
Fragrance like a flower's breath,—
Sweet, demure Elizabeth.

Dimpled cheek and rosy ear,
With the brown hair rippling near,
Where the shadow deepeneth,—
Witching, coy Elizabeth.

Small red lips and rounded chin
Just above her cameo-pin,
Moving gently with her breath,—
Bonnie, fair Elizabeth.

Tiny foot that peepeth out
From beneath her petticoat ;
Ribbon bright that glisteneth,—
Dainty-robed Elizabeth.

MY BLOTTER.

'TIS a dark, stormy night, and it's fast grow-
    ing late ;
  Outside the fog's thick,—the pane's drip-
    ping with water :
But in here my fire burns bright in the grate,
  While I lazily lean o'er my work, on my
    blotter.

Ah, Jennie, my friend, when your mind has
    been pinned
  Down to Logic all day, till your brain seems
    to totter,
What a pleasure it is to fling books to the wind,
  And a moment to lean with your arm on
    your blotter !

And, Jennie, my friend, do you s'pose I can find,
  In this queer, jostling world, where each one
    is a plotter,

Some fair, dainty maiden, whose heart and
    whose mind
Are as pure as the soft, creamy folds of my
    blotter?

Will her smile be as bright, and her heart be as
    true
    As this little bluebird? And her thought
    without spot, or
A shade of deceit? Will her eyes be as blue
    As the jaunty gay ribbon you tied on my
    blotter?

Will her throat be as soft, and as white as the
    snow,
    And her breath be as fragrant as roses' sweet
    otter?—
(The deuce, though, there goes a great blot on
    this, now!
    However, you know it was made for a
    blotter.)

Do you think I will find her? Ah, well, if I do
    Come across, in my travels, some day, this
    fair daughter,

I'll lay my heart down at her feet.   Let you know
   If I meet with success, by a note, from my
   blotter.

JEN.

A JAUNTY white hat, of outrageous size ;
And a pair of those mischievous jet-black
   eyes
That were made to bewilder the sons of men ;
And the sauciest mouth in the world :—that's
   Jen.

A slim, lithe form, full of girlish grace,
And the most provokingly pretty face
That ever made one turn round again
To look at it twice on the street :—that's Jen.

From the soft white muslin around her throat
To the snow-white edge of her petticoat
You just catch a glimpse of now and then,
An irresistible *dash*,—that's Jen.

A graceful ankle, and tiny foot,
Encased in a dainty Dongola boot ;
And an indescribable style,—but then,
You can't *tell* how a pretty girl looks :—that's
   Jen.

THE SONGS I DO NOT SING.

THEY come to me in my waking,
  In the cold, still midnight air :
They come in the week-day labor,
  They come in the solemn prayer.
They come to me in my reading,
  When the lamp burns dim and low :
They come to me under the gas-light,
  When the music is dreamy and slow.

They come to me in my letters,
  Though they never were written there :
They come from the blue-eyed maiden,
  With the lock of her golden hair.
And I heard one of infinite sweetness
  By the side of a funeral pall ;
And one that I heard in a ball-room
  Was the saddest one of all.

They come like the inspirations
  That came to the prophets of old ;

And they seem like a half-blown rose-bud,
    Just ready to burst and unfold.
And I catch my breath at the sweetness
    Of its odor within my breast;
But I sigh for the measureless beauty
    That never can be expressed.

And I think, " When the day is over,—
    When the work and the care are done, —
I will sing this song in the gloaming,
    To gladden some weary one."
But when I go home, in the twilight,
    There are other things I must do;
And I get no time for the singing
    Until after the evening is through.

And so I go on without singing
    The songs I have felt and heard;
While of all their beauty and sweetness,
    The world knows never a word.
And I say, " It is wrong to keep them,
    For they do not belong to you; —
You are only the harp in the window
    For the breath of the wind to blow through."

And they make, with their heavenly rhythm,
    The poor little songs I have sung
Seem harsh as the jangled chiming
    When the bells are backward rung.
But still the days go without singing,
    Till at last the songs fade, one by one ;
And all I can do, as they vanish,
    Is to sigh for the songs that are gone.

DOWN BY THE BROOK.

I'M down by the brook, Jennie, under the trees,
  Where we used to read in the shade ;
While the stream babbled by, on its old black-
    ened rocks,
  And the light o'er your sun-bonnet played.
And the red moss that grows on the slippery
    stones
  Has the same graceful, feathery look ;
And the willows that bend from the bank, up
    above,
  Are still dipping their leaves in the brook.

The dry grass still grows in the weather-stained
    cracks,
  And the golden-rod bends by the ledge ;
And the foam eddies past, just the same, on the
    stream,
  And the bushes are skirting its edge.

The old seat is still here, with its moss-cush-
    ioned back,
But somehow it isn't the same :
And the noise of the brook has a different sound,
    And seems to be whispering your name.

And so I've been lying here, Jen, half asleep,
    With the leaves and the sun on my book,
And wondering what made it so different then,
    When you were down here by the brook.
And after I've looked at the matter all through,
    With my hat tipped down over my face,
I've reached the conclusion at last, cousin Jen,
    It was *you* that I liked, not the place.

7

DAISIES.

" ' WICH man, poor man, beggar man, sief' —
  Wait till I tell 'ou what 'ou'll be ; —
' Doctor, lawyer, Inzun shief,'
  'Ou couldn't be *zat* one, don't 'ou see?

' Wich man, poor man, beggar man, sief' —
  Aren't 'ou glad it isn't zat one?
' Doctor, lawyer, Inzun shief,' —
  Wait a minute, I's almost done.

' Wich man' — zats the lastest one,
  So zat is what 'ou's doing to be.

' Wich man, poor man, beggar man, sief' —
  I dess I must see who'll marry me :
' Doctor, lawyer, Inzun shief,'
  Who do 'ou 'spose it's doing to be?

' Wich man ' — why, it tums ze same !
  I doesn't see how zat can be ! —
O, 'es, I does, — it's dest as plain, —
  O' course it means *'ou'll* marry *me*."

LINES,

WRITTEN ON A BIRCH-BARK CUP.

CRYSTAL cup or golden goblet
    Were not for your lips too fair ;
Yet this little birchen dipper
    Claims at least one virtue rare :
For before your ruby lip
O'er its raveled edge did dip,
    On the mountain streamlet's bank,
    From it never mortal drank.

A LETTER.

WE'RE up at the cottage, Jen, spending a
week ;
Aunt Hattie and Mamie are here :
The breeze is as fresh on the lake as it was
That day you were up here last year ;
We wear our old clothes in the same reckless
way
All day long,— "sans disgrace et sans fear" ;
I feel the old lazy, luxurious ease ;
But, Jen,— O, I wish you were here !

The ripples still break on the sand by the beach,
And the boat's keel still grates on the stones ;
The hammock still swings 'neath the trees in the
grove,
And we still pelt each other with cones :
The golden-rod still grows as bright by the road,
And the "natives" still prowl 'round as
near ;

Our wet bathing-suits are still spread in the
    sun,—
  O, Jen,—but I wish you were here !

The maple trees stand by the rail, as of old,
    And their branches bend low o'er the rocks ;
And the same mingled sunshine and shade from
    their leaves
    Still flecks the veranda's broad walks ;
We still eat our dinners from forks with two
    tines,
    As we did that day up here last year,
When I helped you to salad five times in one
    meal,—
  O, Jen,—well, I wish you were here !

MY TENNIS HAT.

TRIOLET.

SHE wore my tennis hat that day,
   As she stood there beside the net;
   And Hebe could not match the way
She wore my tennis hat that day:
I hear her still, call " Love All — Play ! "
But though she played against me,— yet
She wore my tennis hat that day,
   As she stood there beside the net !

MY POLO CAP.

IT is faded and worn, and the weather
  Has turned it a rather dull red ;
But I have the old feeling of freedom
  When I put it round here on my head.

It brings back those sets of Lawn Tennis
  Kate Harding and I used to play ;
And how she would get the " advantage "
  In a most unaccountable way.

I wore it that day at the races,
  When we paddled in second-best,
While Gordon led off by two boat-lengths
  And we were as far from the rest.

And then, on that last Friday evening,
  When I came back from yachting with Ray
And knew I must leave Monday morning,
  As college commenced the next day ; —

How, when I called over at " Edgemere,"
   I found Jen was up at the lake
For a week,— when I'd just left the fellows
   And pawned my last day for her sake.

Next morning I started to tramp it,
   With shot-gun and rod for excuse ;
And Madge took me up in her dog-cart
   As far as the road was in use.

And then I had eight miles of tramping ;
   But somehow it didn't seem long,
As I gave a fresh tip to my polo,
   And whistled an old college song.

Ah, that afternoon, I remember,
   As I sat on the rocks at her side,—
Just far enough off from the cottage,
   While Fan kept discreetly aside,—

How I told Jen of all my love-troubles, —
   How Flo and I'd broken,— " for good " :
And she gave advice like a Mentor,
   And scolded me out of my " mood."

And then how I made that old boat go,
  As we rowed down the lake to the mills;
While the water reflected the sunset
  That was fading out, over the hills.

Then we waited and let the Professor
  Overtake us, at last, in his birch,
And I got aboard like a greenhorn,
  And gave him a terrible lurch.

And then I watched Jen turn the boat round,
  And the water and sunset-tints blend:
And looked back and waved my old polo
  As we paddled the birch round the bend.

And the long homeward tramp in the evening,
  And what I was thinking of then;—
The present, the past, and the future,—
  The lake, and the day, and of Jen.

And as I strode on down the roadside,
  With the dew and the dust on my shoes,
How squarely I braced up my shoulders,
  No one but my old polo knows.

Well, that was my last tramp that summer,—
All summers must come to an end ;
But still, when I put on my polo
It seems like an old, trusted friend.

AN AUTUMN HYMN.

FROM jeweled censers rich and fair,
Swung low by breath of perfumed air,
The flowers wet with morning dew
Their incense raise, O Lord to you.

The gorgeous clouds of light that lie
Along the glowing western sky ; —
The falling leaf's most brilliant hue ; —
Were painted, Lord of Light, by you.

O Lord of Life, within our hearts
The sense of all thy bounty starts ;
With flowers, leaves, and sky, we too
Would raise, O Lord, our voice to you.

FLOWERS.

W E send them to a child-friend : — send them
    still to one
  Whom years and sorrow have left bowed
    and lonely :
To those with whom acquaintance has but just
    begun,
  And to our best and dearest, we send only —
    Flowers.

We send them to a friend in luxury and need :
  We send them for the burial and the wed-
    ding : —
It is the same we send the living and the dead.
  We send to those who bitter tears are shed-
    ding,—
    Flowers.

We send them to a lady friend before the ball :
  We send them to our relatives,— our lover :

And yet they say the very word we mean to all.
What thoughts of grief, joy, sorrow, love, hang over
Flowers !

INSPIRATIONS.

TELL me not the ancient prophets
    Came of an extinguished line ; —
That they left no true descendants
    Who are touched with flame divine.

Many an unknown, unnamed singer
    Feels a spirit loose his tongue, —
Feels the power within to utter
    Psalms and poems never sung.

Woe to him who such inbreathings
    Deigns to slight, or dares neglect ; —
Or, beneath the smouldering ashes,
    Fails the god-spark to detect.

'Tis a message sent from Heaven, —
    You, a messenger, at best :
Till his errand is delivered
    May no message-bearer rest.

Listen to the heaven-sent message,
　　Be you poet, painter, priest,—
Mould it in your noblest image,
　　Send it forth unscarred, at least.

You may not the final reader
　　Of your sealed dispatches know ;
You may only catch a glimmer
　　Of the Jove-sent fire's glow :

But some heart is surely waiting
　　Your dispatches to receive : —
That your post is worth a life-long
　　Struggle, you may well believe.

A CLOUDY MORNING IN THE COUNTRY.

AURORA leaves her early couch
And mounts the sky in haste, to vouch
  For Sol's returning light.
Her crimson banners herald forth
To denizens of heaven and earth
  The banishment of Night.

The early wight whose weary eyes
Behold her signals in the skies,
  And flaunting streamers gay,
Would fain assay to prophesy
(And give experience the lie)
  " A pleasant day to-day."

But ere the day is well begun
A cold, gray mist shuts out the sun,—
  The clouds are dark and blue.
The farmer stands and looks around,—
On mist and cloud and sky and ground
  In doubt what best to do.

Dead leaves shake on the naked trees,
And on the cheerless, chilly breeze
    Stray flakes go floating past.
  The air seems close,—the hours lag by,—
A leaden pall shuts out the sky : —
    By noon 'tis snowing fast.

9

THE ANGELUS BELL.

LISTEN, my soul! 'tis the Angelus bell
      Dolefully, soulfully tolling its knell;
Tolling a knell for the dying day : —
Calling to sinners to stop and pray,—
Pray for forgiveness, and peace, and rest,
Pray to the Mother of Christ, the Blest;
  " *Ave Sanctissima, ora pro nobis,*"
  Now and when death is near, "*ora pro
  nobis.*"

Think what a burden of sin and crime,
Rolls from the world at the Angelus time,
Up through the peaceful evening air,
Floats into space, on the wings of prayer!
Think of the hearts and the heads bowed
      low,
Touched by the tints of the sunset's glow :
Think of the endless wave of prayer
That rolls round the earth in the twilight
      air !

May it not be that the Saints above
Pause and gaze earthward with looks of love,
As up through the infinite depths of air
Comes floating the incense of evening prayer,
Laden with cares and sins forgiven ; —
Promised pardon and hopes of Heaven,
And the longing sighs that of old age tell ;
And the far-away sound of the Angelus
    bell ?

Then pause, my soul, as the sun goes down
On the fair, green fields and the busy town ;
Pause and think of the day that is gone,—
The words that are spoken, the deeds that
    are done,—
Pause and pray for forgiveness and rest,
And a home at last with the Mother Blest.
For the day shall come when thine earthly
    ear,
No longer the Angelus bell shall hear :
But thou shalt rise on its tolling knell.
Then listen ! my soul, to the Angelus bell !

A BIRTHDAY WISH.

MAY the stars that looked down on thy
      birthday,
  Grow bright as the autumns roll by :
And adding each year still a new one,
  Like jewels in crystals on high,
Shine forth in a fair constellation
  To brighten thy life's evening sky.

ODE

FOR THE NIGHT BEFORE A BIRTHDAY.

COME, brighten the fire, and fill up the
    glasses !
  Let us shorten the evening with laughter
    and song :
Here's a health to Old Time,— let us drink
    as he passes,
  And wish him good luck as he hurries
    along.

Another year's dead, then ; well, peace to
    its ashes !
  May its bones be at rest with its ances-
    tors' dust.
But why should I mourn, or a tear wet the
    lashes,
  That twelve months more are past? I
    am wiser, I trust.

Old Time's an old miser, with all of his
  treasures :
  'Tis but slowly he doles out our joys and
  our pains.
On the whole, though, he's fair ;— for all
  griefs there are pleasures,
  And he brings us no loss that has not its
  own gains.

Though the year that is past has been full of
  lost chances,—
  Opportunities wasted, by night and by
  day,—
Yet why should I follow its form with sad
  glances
  As it turns the last corner, and hurries
  away ?

Let us laugh while youth lasts ; — time
  enough to be dreary
  When its flowers have faded, its leaves
  have grown brown ;
Time enough to be sad when the heart has
  grown weary
  Of bearing the burden 'twould gladly lay
  down.

Then brighten the fire, and fill up the glasses !
 Let us drown all such thoughts with a
  laugh and a song :
Here's a toast to Old Time,— let us
 drink as he passes,
And hail the old chap as he shuffles
 along.

I say, Father Time,— look alive,— turn your
 glass there : —
 The sand's all run out,— you'll get left
  some fine day !
I forgot : —" Local Time,"— not the " Stand-
 ard " : — I pass : — there,
 I'm glad *you* keep on in the old-fashioned
  way.

Well, well, time wags on ; and for one, I'm
 glad of it : —
 To be, all one's life, just so old,— what a
  bore !
Let them call back their childhood who can,
 and who love it,—
 I'm content that my mumps and my
  measles are o'er.

But, friends, it is late, and I see you are
yawning : —
The bell on the steeple, the clock on the
wall,
Say the evening is past, and day soon will
be dawning.
We must part, or we'll hear shrill old
Chanticleer's call.

Yes Time, it is said (and 'tis true), works
great changes,—
Weaves the world in the web of a magi-
cal spell : —
But there's none that's more queer than the
trick where he ranges
From one year to the next at the stroke
of a bell.

But once more by the fire let us fill up our
glasses,—
Join once more in the laugh, the familiar
old song !
Here's the health of Old Time ; — let us
drink as he passes,
And cheer his old bones as he hobbles
along.

And now, friends, good-night.   Yes, I know
    your kind wishes,
  And I thank you for them from the depth
    of my heart :
One true word of a friend is worth all of
    Love's kisses.
  Let us shake hands all round with a will,
    ere we part,—

But no wishes to-night : let them wait till
    to-morrow ;
  They will be all the better, and,— hark !
    what was that?
Yes, the bell tolling midnight.   For joy or
    for sorrow
  Another year's come, like a silent winged
    bat.

Pleasant dreams and sound sleep, and clear
    heads in the morning ;
  I must sit up a while, with my thoughts,
    ere I go,
And make good resolves for the year that is
    dawning,
  Ere the daylight creeps in where the fire
    burns low.

II

OTHER VERSES

JUST A SOCIETY GIRL.

SHE is no simple village lass,
  The maiden of my singing:
No country town or rustic lane
  With praise of her is ringing.

No wayside flower is she, that grows
  'Mid tangled leaves and grasses;
No blue-bell meek, or frail wild-rose,
  That he may pluck who passes.

Let poets sing of rustic grace,
  Of simple lives and pleasures:—
They who find gems in buttercups
  Are welcome to their treasures.

They seem to think, these poet-chaps,
  Who sing of flowing tresses,
That all the maids worth singing of
  Are found in homespun dresses.

I sing of one whose life goes round
  Like one of her own glances,—
A constant whirl of dinners, teas,
  Of flowers, bouquets and dances.

A life made up of concerts, plays,
  Of satins, gloves and laces;
Of calls and cards, of parties, balls,
  And endless rows of faces.

No knowledge of great Nature's laws
  This maid of mine professes:
But, oh, the wealth of worldly lore
  Her woman's heart possesses!

She knows the power that money brings,—
  Its pride, its greed, its passion:
She knows the folly and the good
  That rule the world of fashion.

But though she knows what wealth can give,—
  Its pleasures and its sinning,—
It only makes her seem more fair,
  And doubly worth the winning.

Then let them sing, these poet-fools,
  Their rustic maids and lasses:
I'll sing my winter rose, that blooms
  Beneath the green-house glasses.

But still I know this maid of mine,
  Whose praises I am ringing,
May fail to smile on me at last
  To thank me for my singing.

Too well, alas, may this be true;
  Fair maids are ofttimes wary;
And Jacqueminots are not for him
  Who sings, in February.

But still I yield the palm to none:
  "Faint heart ne'er won fair lady:"
And if need be, I'll wait and sing
  Till youth has lost its heyday.

And if, at last, perchance, the prize
  I lose, with all my striving,
Still shall my praises of her ring,
  All fruitless hopes surviving.

And though this hot-house bud of mine
  Should not be for my wearing,
Still will I dare to hope and be
  The better for the daring.

SAINT VALENTINE'S DAY.

IN those chivalrous days, when the bold troub-
  adours
Caught cold 'neath the windows of fair ladies'
  bowers;
When the knights-errant brave, with long
  plumes in their caps,
Suffered tumbles and bruises and other mis-
  · haps,
To show their devotion,— and good clothes
  as well,—
'Twas a deed for the ballads of minstrels to
  tell
How Sir What's-his-name did his compli-
  ments pay
Lady So-and-so fair, on Saint Valentine's day.
But all that is past. In our commonplace time
Ladies laugh at the wight who indulges in
  rhyme;
Serenades are old-fashioned, wearing plumes
  out of style,

And the last of the troubadours dead a long
    while.
Only ballads and legends of such things re-
    main ;
Yet ballads and legends are not all in vain,
For if you'd a lady a compliment pay,
You must send her a card on Saint Valentine's
    day.

WITH A MS. BOOK.

THESE few little "Songs from the Seasons,"
 I send you, fair cousin of mine,—
Poor stray little rhymes without reasons,—
 In charge of Saint Valentine.

They come from the land of the snow-drift,
 The east-wind, the frost and the sleet,
Where the full moon looks down through the
 cloud-rift
 On the snow-covered house-tops and street:

Where the trees in the forests are bending
 'Neath the weight of their burdens of
 snow;
Where the fast-frozen rivers are sending
 Their floods through the ice-caves below:—

To you, in your bright Colorado,
 Where the valleys lie warm in the sun, —
In your fair western new El Dorado,
 More rich than the old fabled one.

And perhaps they may bring you some token
 From the land of your birth and your
  youth : —
Some link in the chain that is broken,
 Some word you may feel as the truth.

Perhaps you may catch some faint shimmer
 Of those bright summer skies over head,
Whose lights on the fair lake still glimmer,
 Though the lilies we pulled may be dead.

Though, perchance, they may hold no rich ·
  treasures
 Of wisdom, I trust there may lie,
Somewhere in my poor little measures —
 (*How* poor none can know better than I),

Some thought that is true the world over :
 For, whatever, its fashion or name,
The thought that is dear to the lover,
 Is always and ever the same.

Accept, then, these " Songs from the Sea-
  sons,"
 O fair Western cousin of mine ;
And ask not for rhythm or reasons ·
 In the month of Saint Valentine.

LOST YOUTH.

IN sunny Rockport by the sea
The world looked bright to you and me,
    In that first summer, long ago,
    When one delicious mellow glow,—
Which you and I may find no more,—
Bathed rocks and mountains, sea and shore :
    And Youth was Now to you and me
    In sunny Rockport by the sea.

Fair hillside Rockport by the sea !
Familiar are its rocks to me :
    Familiar are its mountain sides,
    Its ebbing and its flowing tides :
And every rock and tree we knew
Brings thronging memories filled with you,—
    What might have been for you and me
    In hillside Rockport by the sea.

The days have come, the days have gone,
While I have wandered here alone :

And Youth, and Hope, and Joy, and you,
Seem but as things I never knew.
For all the brightening mist has fled,
And all the hopes of Youth are dead.
And life looks stern to you and me,
In rugged Rockport by the sea.

EVENING ON THE HARBOR.

A S I drift in my boat on the harbor,
In the calm of the summer night,
The moon in the arms of the crescent
Floods all with its misty light.

The water reflects the moonbeams
In a wavy, twisted band,
Like a mirror of polished metal
From some distant Eastern land.

No sound but the click of a rowlock,
And the measured dip of an oar,
And the lisping plash of the ripples,
As they break on the western shore.

The lights in the hillside village
Are fading into the night;
But a kiln, with its flaming furnace,
Gleams out with a ruddy light.

The ships' great forms around me
    Are grim as the jaws of death,
And the gray masts rise like spectres
    That would vanish away at a breath.

The water is smooth and glassy,—
    Its spirit is hushed to rest ;
And 'tis only the swell from the ocean
    That tells of its heaving breast.

O, would that each toiling mortal
    Could feel the calm and rest
That comes with the evening stillness
    To the ocean's troubled breast : —

Could feel that the noise and toiling,
    All day, in the busy town,
Is only the breeze from the ocean,
    And will cease when the sun goes down.

And the waves that are ever tossing,—
    The foam and the plashes of strife,—
Grow calm, and only the surges
    Roll in from the Ocean of Life.

BABY'S SOCKS.

WHAT can I say of the Baby's socks?
　　Poets may sing about golden locks,
　Sparkling eyes and rosy lips,
　Soft white hands and finger-tips,
But whoever wrote of a baby's socks!

Queer little bag of white and blue,—
　Who would have thought it was meant
　　for a shoe?
(I never should, I am sure, should you,
　If it hadn't been that there were two?)

By and by, when the baby walks,
　She'll need something stouter than
　　worsted socks,
For she'll find that the road is full of rocks,
　And she'll wish, sometimes, I am will-
　　ing to bet,
　She were back in her babyhood's stock-
　　ings yet;—

Back in her mother's arms once more,
  Kicking her feet on the the carpeted floor.

For by and by, as the years roll on,
And babyhood's socks are long outgrown,
And she goes out in the world alone,
  She'll find it isn't so easy to walk
  By half as you'd think to hear some
  folks talk.

For the path is rough, and the road is
  long,
And its awfully hard to tell right from
  wrong,
  But if she will only try to keep
  Where she *thinks* is right, though the
  road is steep
She'll find that at last it will lead her out
Where the way is plain, and she need not
  doubt.

EASTER DAY.

WHEN the sun is bright and fair,
   And the sunshine fills the air :
When the gentle breath of Spring
Does the yellow crocus bring,
Peeping through the melting snow,
From its winter bed below :
When the skies above seem glad,
And no earthly thing is sad,
But the whole world's blithe and gay,—
Then, you know, 'tis Easter Day.

When each face with smiles is decked,
When the colors bright reflect
All the tints the rainbow knows :
When each heart with joy o'erflows,
And each passer on the street,
Pausing, stops, his friend to greet :
When the church is decked with flowers,—
Font and altar fairy bowers :—

When the glad chime's joyous note
Swelling through the air doth float,
To all men it seems to say,
" This, you know, is Easter Day."

When the Saviour, long ago,
In the tomb was lying low,
Then an Angel, bright as day,
Rolled the sealed stone away.
This is why the world is glad,
Why no mortal can be sad,
Why the crocus lifts its head ;
For the Saviour, from the dead,
On that ever blessed morn,
In the early coming dawn,
When the light was cold and gray,—
Rose, you know, on Easter Day.

CARDS.

WE have cards for a wedding, and cards for
   a call,
For Christmas, and New Year's, and Easter,
   and all :
We have cards for a birthday, and cards for
   a prize ;
We have cards every shape, every color and
   size :
Our pious friends give us a lecture and say
"Never play games at cards,—you will rue it
   some day ;"
And while with their preaching we're still
   feeling vexed
They turn round and give us a *card*, with
   a text !
We have cards in the mail, — they come
   thicker than showers ;
And when we are sending a young lady
   flowers

'Tis a card we put in, to express our re-
    gards : —
I 'faith, is this world made of nothing but
    cards?

ECHO.

A PRETTY maiden that I know
  Was telling Echo 'bout her beau.
" He calls my nose a pug," she said,
" And says my hair is almost red ;
Now, don't you think he's rather dainty ? "
Familiar Echo answers, " Ain't he ? "

" I don't believe he cares for me
As much as Rover does," said she ;
"If I should fall into the sea,
How far, to save me, think, would he
Rush boldly through the briny deep ? "
Sarcastic Echo says, "Knee deep ! "

" But tell me, Echo, what to do ;
I couldn't send him off, could you ?
I rather guess I'll let him come,
And make him think I love him *some*.
I'll not be very unjust so."
And Echo acquiesced, " Just so ! "

NO GO.

A H, my pretty, dainty Martha,
    Don't you know I love you, say?
Will you let me come a-wooing?
    Pretty Martha answered, Nay.

Would you like to have me leave you,
    Go and leave you all the day,
Go and woo some other maiden?
    Pretty Martha answered, Yea.

But if I should stay and love you,
    Come and woo you all the day,
Don't you think you'd take your lover?—
    Pretty Martha walked away.

A REMEMBRANCE.

INTENDED TO HAVE BEEN SENT TO A YOUNG
LADY.

A S each Autumn's breath the same colors
Brings back to the leaves on the trees,
Though the leaves are not really the same ones
That fluttered in last Autumn's breeze ;

So to me the chill winds of November,
As they whistle and whirl in the street,
Bring a thought of the daintiest maiden
It was e'er my good fortune to meet.

We met in the drear, early winter ;
She was gone while the snow was still white ;
But she left in my memory a picture
That will ever be charming and bright.

If you chance, anywhere in your wanderings,
To meet with the maiden, my friend,

Please wish her the season's best wishes,—
  Good things and good luck without end.

VERSE FOUND ADDED ON THE AUTHOR'S MAN-
USCRIPT.

Try it again, and perhaps you'll do better ;
  Cut it down to one verse ;
Try it again, and perhaps you'll do better,
  You *couldn't* do worse.

REMEMBRANCES.

I LITTLE did think, fair Jennie,
  That morn when we met by the lake,
Of the lasting place, through years to come,
  That you in my thoughts would take.

And little I thought, fair Jennie,
  That day by the murmuring brook,
That I should for years remember
  Each motion and word and look.

And little we thought, fair Jennie,
  When we climbed on the mountain's side,
How often would forest and mountain
  Be mirrored in memory's tide.

I little did think, fair Jennie,
  In the gloam of twilight air,
By the porch where the woodbine was growing,
  How long I should linger there.

But the lake, and the brook, and the mountain,
　Have never since then been the same,
And still in the gloam of the twilight,
　My heart is repeating your name.

WHY?

WHY is it that whene'er I meet,
    Whene'er I pass upon the street,
One dainty maiden that I know,
My little wits desert me so?.

Is it the dimple in her cheek
That holds me so I cannot speak?
Is it her ribbon, or her pin,
That prickles so, my heart within?

Is it some one, or all of these,
That doth my 'wildered senses tease,
So that I know not what to do?
O dear! I cannot tell; can you?

IVY ODE.

TO THE CLASS OF '85, BATES COLLEGE, JUNE 11, 1884.

RICH, glossy and bright are the Ivy's green
leaves,
  And its branches are rugged and strong ;
Firm, twisted and strong is the web that it weaves
  As its climbers creep slowly along.
  It clings to the last, where its roots have once
    been,
  And age but enriches and deepens its green.

Rich, glowing and bright is a strong friendship
    true,
  And its grasp is as lasting as steel,
Its words weave their meshes around all we do,
  As the years from our life's spool unreel.
  And firmly it clings with its strong youthful
    hold,

While age but enriches its bright burnished
   gold.

Then bury our Ivy's roots deep in the earth,
   Let us cherish each shoot as it twines,
For the Ivy shall symbol our friendship's true
      worth,
   As its roots in our hearts its entwines,
   And higher and higher its branches shall go,
   While years in our friendship no changes
      shall know.

FETTERS.

TELL me not of fetters
    For a maiden's hand;
But a toy to her is
    Every golden band.
Tell me not of fetters
    For a maiden's heart;
Like a broken bow-string,
    Vows she snaps apart.

Once I wooed a maiden,—
    Wooed her with a zeal
Full of love and passion,
    Naught but youth can feel.
And she met my wooing
    With a heart of love,
Fervent as a mother's,
    Pure as heaven above.

On a maiden's finger
    Once I slipped a ring,

Set with pearl and turquoise,
  Airy, fragile thing!
Pearls and azure turquoise,
  Like a summer sky:—
Firmer than our love, that
  We thought ne'er could die!

Then I locked a bracelet
  Round her willing wrist;
And we locked on with it
  Lovers' vows, I wist.
But the golden fetter
  Proved as light as air,
No more held the maiden
  Than a silken hair.

Then I round her finger,
  E'er so hard to hold,
Placed a narrow circlet
  Of plain, yellow gold,
Sealed it with a diamond's
  Flashing rays of light:—
Still the jewel glistens
  Than our love more bright.

Let them lie and tarnish
In their velvet case !
Bound will I be never
To a pretty face.
Let the vows be buried
Deeply in my heart ;
And when I forget them,
Sting me with their smart.

"SWEET CAPORAL."

WHEN all the world seems out of rhyme,
　　The idle day but wasted time,
The evening like a farce played out;
While in my mind crowds many a doubt;
When disappointments fill the air;
When friends prove false and maids unfair;
When love affairs look dark and blue,
And unpaid tailors' bills come due:—
Then, then, my cigarette I light,
And all my troubles take their flight.
And, as its glowing end I watch,
Like some red, sympathetic torch,
Responsive to my every mood,
To lighten my disquietude;
The clouds roll by, the moon sails out,
And banishes all shade and doubt.
So, in my mind doubt clears away,
And calmer thoughts and words hold sway.
And as the fragrant smoke ascends,
And with the evening stillness blends,

A burden seems to roll away,—
The cares and trials of the day.
Then all the world again looks bright,
And unpaid tailors' bills seem light
As ashes from my cigarette,
And I forget that I'm in debt,
While love affairs look bright once more,
Which but a little while before
    Had seemed so dark and squally.
So, in my hammock here I lie,
Beneath the pale blue moonlit sky,
    And bless Sir Walter Raleigh.

A PUFF OF SMOKE.

WHEN the world seems all a blur
    And grim thoughts crowd thick around ;
When Youth's dead hopes thickly fall
    As the leaves on Autumn's ground,
Past griefs flit before me :—Whew !
    Clouds of fragrant smoke hide all.

Out of doors one dismal blur,
    Fog clings to the dripping pane,
But within my study bright,
    Thicker than the fog or rain
Float the fragrant smoke clouds :—Whew !
    Hiding all the world from sight !

Has the great world's deafening whir
    Turned me from walks with books ?
Disappointments filled the day ?
    Do some fair one's scornful looks
Rankle in my mind still ?—Whew !
    Thus I blow them all away.

Am I sad with thought of *her*,
  Loved and lost for many a day,—
Thoughts of all that might have been?
  Like a spectre, gaunt and gray,
Does her vision haunt me?—Whew!
  One good puff hides all the scene.

Do I feel my pulses stir
  To be mingling in the strife,
'Neath the banner's stripes unfurled,—
  Seek for broader fields of life,
Seek a chance for action?—Whew!
  In that cloud floats all the world.

THE SEASONS.

SPRING.

B^{REEZE,} Trees,
Freeze,
Sneeze ;
A youth and maiden off a-Maying.

SUMMER.

A lake,
A snake,
Sun-bake,
Head-ache ;
Big hotel bills papas are paying.

AUTUMN.

Twinkling stars,
Rustic bars,
Shrewd mammas ;
"Ask papa's
Consent," some pretty lips are saying.

WINTER.

A crowded hall,
A fancy ball,
A stupid call,
And—that is all!
The same old game they all are playing.

THE POET AND THE SINGER.

SHE sang that night in the party's whirl,
  'Neath the glare of the chandelier,
And the poet he listened with all his might,
  And held his breath to hear.

His rival he stood on her right hand,
  With that graceful pose he had,
And he turned her page with a negligent air
  That drove the poor poet mad.

And they sang together, as they stood there,
  In the glare of the chandelier ;
And the poet he fretted and fumed and fussed,
  But he could not choose but hear.

And he said to himself, " That song she sings
  Is as old as the art of rhymes,
And every dabbler who sings at all
  Has sung it an hundred times.

15

She ought not to be singing those worn-out songs
  That were here when the Mastodons were ;
The song that she sings should be like her dress,
  And suited alone for her."

And he said to himself, "I will write her a song,
  This night, when the party is o'er,
That she shall sing for the very first time
  As never she sang before."

So the poet went home to his room that night,
  When the hum of the party was o'er,
And he wrote a song that was better far
  Than he ever had written before :

A song of love, and a warrior bold,
  And a maiden who loved a knight,
A knight who vanquished his rival's lance
  In the midst of the thickest of the fight.

And he set the words to an old faint air
  That the troubadour's strings had rung,
That had laid for hundreds of years at least
  In its parchment roll, unsung.

And he said, "She will sing my song to-night,
 In the glare of the chandelier,
And the people will murmur their praise of the
  song,
 And my rival he needs must hear."

But when she sung his song that night,
 In the glare of the chandelier,
His rival he stood on her right hand,
 And the poet could not but hear.

And they sang together that song of his,
 That he had written for her,
And he wished it was buried beneath the sea,
 And as dead as the Mastodons were.

And the people they murmured their soft, low
  praise,
 When the song and singers were through,
And some, they murmured the poet's name,
 That to him there were praises due.

But mostly they praised the singers' skill,
 As they stood 'neath the chandelier,
And his rival, he smiled with a broad, bland
  smile,
 And the poet could not but hear,

But when he complained to her that she
  Had not sung him his song alone,
She only laughed and said, "Oh, well,
  It was better for two than one."

He said it was written for her to sing,
  For her, and for her alone,
And he wanted no lips to utter the words,
  But only hers and his own.

But she only laughed and shook her head,
  And said, as she turned to go,
With a voice like the sound of a silver bell,
  " *You* couldn't have *sung* it, you know ! "

" *He* could not have written it, either," he cried,
  But she laughed, like a silver bell,
"It doesn't much matter who writes the song,"
  She said, "If it's only sung well."

           *   *   *   *   *   *   *

The poet went home to his room that night,
  And vowed he would write no more,
For his song had but bettered his rival's case,
  And made his own worse than before.

The moral is plain. If you want in this world
  To help your own cause along,
Don't try to furnish the brains, but learn
  To sing some one else's song.

LIFE'S DAY.

MORNING dawns; the earth is•bright,
With the sun's returning light,
And his golden, broadened ray
Cheers the land throughout the day;
Till, as twilight fills the air
With its mystery soft and fair,
Magic-like, the moonlight's ray
Turns the earth to silver-gray.

So, in youth, the cheek is red,
Sunshine nestles on the head;
While, though life's long working day,
Light and shade alternate stray,
Till old age, with creeping pace,
Draws its lines upon the face;
Then some unseen magic ray
Turns the hair to silver-gray.

COLORS.

KNIGHTS of old, in bloody fray,
Wore fair ladies' colors gay ;
And to keep them from the dust,
Gave full many a well-aimed thrust.

Women still may color give
To the age in which they live ;
To men's thoughts and acts give tone,
By the tenor of their own.

CHIVALRY.

GO search through History's pages bright
    For valiant feat of armed knight,
Read all her storied annals hold,
Of warlike deeds of men of old,
Whose light still down the ages shines.
But could you read between the lines,
In all the list you'd find not one
That was not for some woman done.

I WONDER.

I WONDER if she guesses it,
  My little lady fine ;
Her picture ne'er expresses it,
  This photograph of mine.

She sits up there and looks at me,
  Upon the mantel high,
(Meanwhile chum's throwing books at me,
  Because I don't reply.)

She little knows what vows I make
  Before this shrine of her's,
And could she see the bows I make,
  She call me mad, or worse.

I wonder if she dreams of it,
  If ever, through her mind,
Go floating stray, faint gleams of it,
  Like straws that show the wind.

I sing my little songs to her,
　Poor, witty, long, or terse ;
Each trifle that belongs to her
　I weave into my verse.

She takes them all so prettily,
　I think she must have guessed ;
Then turns them off as wittily
　As though 'twere all in jest.

I wonder if she heeds them all,
　And if she half divines
The meanings, as she reads them all,
　I write between the lines.

Would she accept—refuse it all
　If she should guess, who knows?
And would I gain, or lose it all,
　If I should speak in prose?